BERCHICK

BERCHICK

Story by
Esther Silverstein Blanc

Pictures by
Tennessee Dixon

VOLCANO
·PRESS·

Volcano, California

Library of Congress Cataloging-in-Publication Data
Blanc, Esther Silverstein, 1913-
     Berchick, my mother's horse/by Esther Silverstein Blanc:
illustrated by Tennessee Dixon.

     Summary: Homesteading in Wyoming in the early 1900's, a Jewish
mother develops an unusual relationship with a colt she adopts named
Berchick.
     ISBN   0-912078-81-2
     [1. Horses – Fiction.   2. Jews – United States – Fiction.]
I. Dixon, Tennessee, ill.   II. Title.
PZ7.B586Be 1988
[Fic] – dc19   87-37172
                                                         CIP
                                                         AC

Designed by Dalia Hartman
Printed in Japan
First edition
Production by David Charlsen & Others

Mama was coming across the north pasture
nearest to our house, and had crossed the little
creek on the plank bridge, when she found the
newborn colt standing by the body of his mother.
Mama was carrying a basket with a loaf of bread,
for she had been visiting old Mr. and Mrs. Libby,
and when she did that on a Saturday, Mrs. Libby
gave Mama a loaf of bread to take home.

Mama had not seen the mare before. She did not belong to one of the neighbors. She was lying on her brand side and had died in giving birth to the colt. Mama patted the head of the mare gently and softly and promised that she would take good care of her baby.

Then she and the colt came home together. It was a nice warm day in early spring. The snow had melted, and the colt was able to walk to our house. He was covered in a light brown fur and walked very well for one so young.

My father and brothers were surprised to see the colt. Mama explained everything as she took off her coat, mittens, and hood, put on her apron with the gray and white stripes, and prepared a bottle of warm milk for the new baby. He was made comfortable on an old quilt on the covered back porch of our sod house, and right away he knew how to drink milk out of a bottle with a nipple.

After a while we had fried eggs, cabbage salad, and Mrs. Libby's bread for supper.

"It's really wonderful how happy the Libbys are on their new place." said Mama. "Mr. Libby spends as much time as he likes reading the *Talmud*, and Mrs. Libby keeps busy 'living like in the old country.'"

Papa looked around the table and smiled. "I'm glad for them. For years he worked in a shop and they lived in a tenement. With what they have saved and what their children send them, they have no worries."

Papa said the colt could be named Berchick (which means "little bear" in Yiddish) because his coat was so furry. We all agreed and that became his name at once.

"I must tell the Libbys about Berchick when I go again," said Mama, and then it was time to fix another bottle for him.

"I think Berchick's mother must have wandered off from one of the great ranches to the north of us, where they raise thoroughbreds," said Papa. "It was a good thing that you found him when you did. He surely would have been eaten by the coyotes."

In time Berchick lost his furry coat and emerged sleek and black with a white star on his forehead and some soft white hair near his hoofs. Papa fixed a box stall in the barn for him. Mama sewed a little blanket that slipped over his head and was kept in place by a safety pin. My brothers and I would take him for walks every nice day. He could drink his milk out of a bucket. Mama cooked a warm dish for him called "mash", which he liked very much.

He seemed to be fond of us — my brother Henry, who was ten, most of all. But Berchick was Mama's horse and they both knew it. He followed her faithfully and seemed to understand all of her loving words and simple commands in Yiddish, which Mama spoke better than she did English.

After a time Berchick grew up to be a large horse, but he didn't know that and still behaved like a family pet, which he was. We children stood on apple boxes to groom him. Because he was the oldest, Henry would brush and comb the tallest part of Berchick. Samuel would work on the middle, and since I was the smallest I would do his feet and legs as far up as I could reach.

When Berchick was old enough and Mama said
that his back was strong, we were allowed to ride
him. That is to say, we understood that he would let
us. We rode bareback.

Papa and Mama agreed after some discussion that
Berchick didn't have to work to earn his living.
"There are enough horses already to do the work,"
said Mama, "and Berchick is not the kind of horse to
pull a wagon."

Even though he was grown up and could carry us around on his back, he still liked milk very much. As he was always near Mama when she was milking, he would be given a bucket full of milk occasionally. Mama said she liked watching him blow the milky foam from his lips. If he had milk on his face, she would tidy him up with the corner of her gray-and-white-striped apron.

All the neighbors knew Berchick. When we went visiting, Berchick would go along, wait until the visit was over, walk partway back with us, and then run ahead so that he could meet us at the house.

He seemed to like visiting Mr. and Mrs. Bregar most of all because Mr. Bregar always spoke to him kindly and gave him little treats. Mrs. Bregar liked him too, but she said it made her nervous to know a horse who seemed to understand so much.

"Nonsense," said Mr. Bregar. "Who knows if all horses couldn't be that clever if you started teaching them early enough?"

The Bregars, who had come from Pittsburgh to settle on their homestead, usually agreed about most things, but Mrs. Bregar didn't say "yes" about Berchick, although she gave Mr. Bregar a piece of buttered bread with sugar on top to give to him. Once she was at our house when we were grooming Berchick, and she said it made her nervous to see me going in and out of his legs like that when I was brushing him.

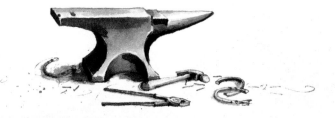

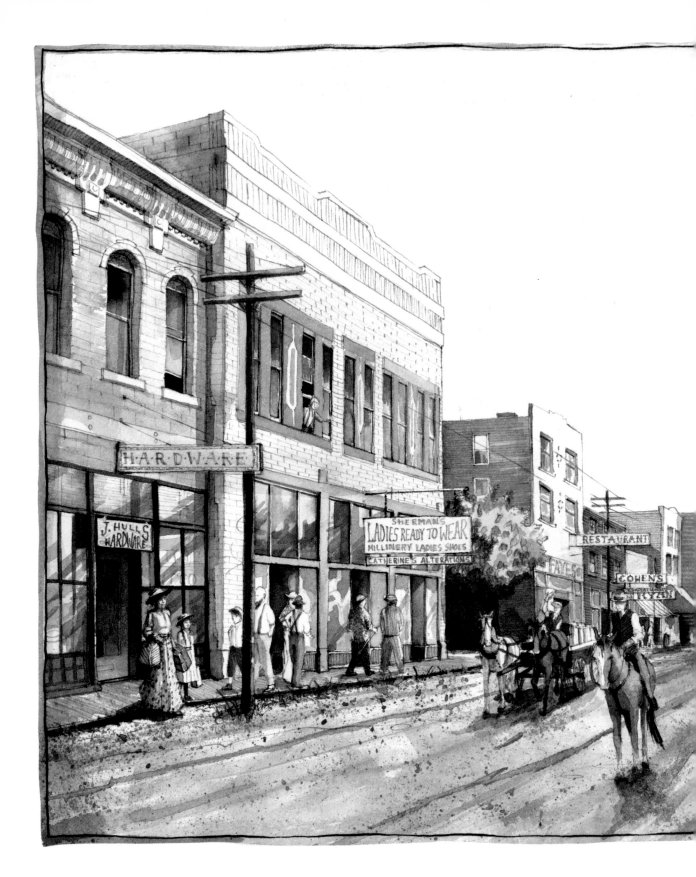

Berchick would trot alongside Nellie, the buggy mare, when Mama rode into town, and waited quietly by the hitching post in front of the store until she came out, placed her parcels in the buggy, and started home. Once within sight of the house Berchick would dash ahead so we knew that she was on the way.

A fence meant nothing to Berchick. He would back off as far as need be and just fly over. We all knew that in his mind a fence was something to jump over.

"So much of the land is open range that it doesn't matter," Papa said. "He stays at home anyway unless he is with one of us. But someday it might matter."

And Mama said, "Simon, by the time it matters, Berchick will be too old to jump fences and will be put in a safe pasture."

Berchick was about three years old when he left home for a month. Mama was very worried. The children missed him. The neighbors asked, "Where is Berchick?" when they came to visit.

Mr. Bregar explained that Berchick was like all other young males, he wanted to see the world. Old Mr. Libby said that Berchick loved us all, especially Mama, and would come home. "For a lost child who returns is cause for rejoicing," said Mr. Libby.

Mrs. Libby was a great comfort to Mama. "I remember the day you found him, poor little orphaned creature, and now he is gone and of course you are worried," she said very kindly.

My brother Samuel, who was quiet most of the time, said, "Even if he has been locked up somewhere, the first time they let him out he will get away. No fence can hold him!"

And that was the way it was. One morning Berchick was home again. I dug some carrots for him from the garden and washed them at the pump, and Mama gave him some *challah* and butter and watermelon for a special treat. After a few days it was as though Berchick had never been away.

Hard times came to our homestead the following two years. One spring, wheat seed cost a great deal. At harvesttime we had a splendid crop and nobody wanted to buy it. Papa told us that we had to leave our homestead and live in town, where Papa would go back to his old trade of being a tailor. All the animals and farm machinery would have to be sold. It was a sad time for us, and parting from our friends was the hardest of all.

In town there was no place to keep a horse, and Berchick had to be sold, too. Mama was grieved, but Berchick trotted along with the other horses when the horse trader came to take them away. We watched from the porch, and when the horses were out of sight, Mama sat down on the step and cried.

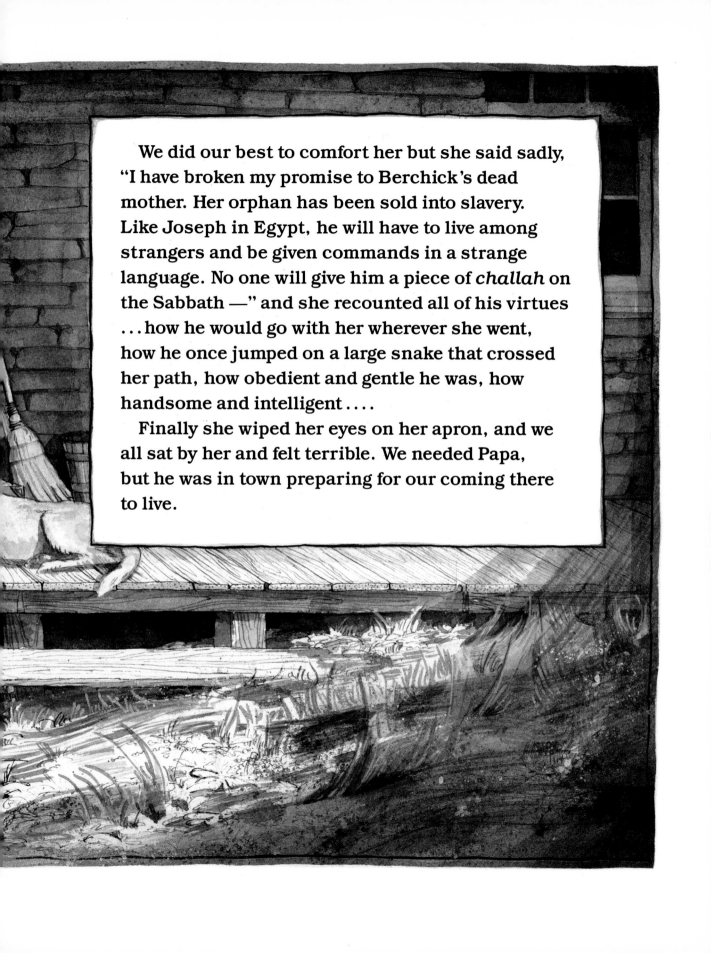

We did our best to comfort her but she said sadly, "I have broken my promise to Berchick's dead mother. Her orphan has been sold into slavery. Like Joseph in Egypt, he will have to live among strangers and be given commands in a strange language. No one will give him a piece of *challah* on the Sabbath —" and she recounted all of his virtues ... how he would go with her wherever she went, how he once jumped on a large snake that crossed her path, how obedient and gentle he was, how handsome and intelligent ....

Finally she wiped her eyes on her apron, and we all sat by her and felt terrible. We needed Papa, but he was in town preparing for our coming there to live.

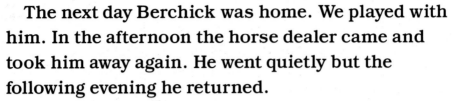

The next day Berchick was home. We played with him. In the afternoon the horse dealer came and took him away again. He went quietly but the following evening he returned.

We could hear Mama talking to him for a long time. It was a clear evening, late in summer, and the stars were out before we went to sleep while Mama stayed with Berchick.

"You had better run away now while you can," she advised him. "We are moving away and we cannot return, I know. Go and make your own way in the world." She petted him and talked and murmured.

In the morning we left early. Papa came for us with a wagon from the livery stable in town. Berchick was gone.

We were all settled in town by November. We children were going to school, each in a grade of his or her own — not all of us in one room with one teacher as it had been in our small school near the homestead.

I liked the old way better. Henry said he could learn more this way. He wanted to be a teacher when he grew up. And Samuel said it didn't matter to him one way or the other because he was going to be a farmer.

Mr. and Mrs. Bregar came for Thanksgiving and brought Mr. and Mrs. Libby. We were all so very happy. Everybody hugged one another. Mrs. Bregar brought me a pink silk hair ribbon, and Mrs. Libby brought two very large loaves of bread.

Mama made European dishes and roasted a large turkey, and we had rice cooked Turkish style, dill pickles, baked squash, and strudel for dessert.

After dinner the grown-ups had coffee and talked. The children listened. Mr. Bregar said he had a surprise. The week before, he had gone up to Laramie Peak to cut wood for the winter and had company the whole time. Berchick was there running with a herd of wild horses. He stayed by Mr. Bregar's wagon and had shared some of his bread and butter.

"How did he look?" asked Mama.

"He seemed strong and well as ever, just like he was when he lived with you," said Mr. Bregar.

"What a *chochim!*" said Papa. "He lives in freedom like a real wild creature."

"That is what is most important," Mama said softly. "It is most important of all."

About the author

Esther Silverstein Blanc was born in 1913, on a homestead in Goshen County, Wyoming. Her parents, Simon and Gazella, had moved west to settle on 160 acres of unbroken prairie, where they built their sturdy dry sod house.

Other Jewish families had also settled in the area, and as a child Esther remembers being told that the philanthropic Baron de Hirsch fund had aided many of them in moving west from Pittsburgh, Pennsylvania. Later, the family moved to Mitchell, Nebraska, where Esther graduated from high school in 1931. In 1934, she moved to San Francisco to become a registered nurse.

Her nursing experiences include a year in a front-line operating room during the Spanish Civil War, and during World War II she served as a second lieutenant in the U.S. Army Nurse Corps.

In 1972 she obtained a Ph.D. in the history of medicine, which she taught at the University of California, San Francisco, for many years.

She retired in 1984, and is now engaged in a social and historical study of Charles Darwin and his associates.

About the illustrator

Tennessee Dixon says, "I've a long-standing affinity with the Great Plains region—from the vast grasslands to the Black Hills. What a treat to have my first children's book set in the country so close to my heart. Thanks to those who helped me along the way, including the staff at the Homesteaders Museum in Torrington, Wyoming, and the North Platt Valley Museum in Gering, Nebraska."

GLOSSARY

Challah: A braided loaf of bread, usually baked for the Sabbath.
Chochim: A wise, clever person—a people's sage.
Talmud: Writings which constitute Jewish civil and religious law.

Temple Israel

Minneapolis, Minnesota

IN HONOR OF THE 80TH BIRTHDAY
OF
ROSE SCHLEIFF
BY
HER FRIENDS